The Farm Stand Mystery

by Shaunda Wenger
illustrated by Jeff Ebbeler

Meet the Characters

Dad

Matt

Nora

Penny Porto

Dad says, "Kids, let's pick the vegetables. I think we will have the best farm stand ever."

Matt picks 67 peppers. Nora picks 84 tomatoes. Dad looks at the lettuce. "I have 33 heads of lettuce," says Dad.

Nora fills her baskets with tomatoes.
Matt fills his bags with peppers.
Dad fills his boxes with lettuce.

Dad, Nora, and Matt drive
to the farm stand. *Bounce! Plop!*
Some vegetables fall off the truck.

Dad, Nora, and Matt finally get to the farm stand. They put the vegetables on the table. Nora counts 11 tomatoes. Matt counts 12 peppers. How many vegetables are missing?

"I do not think we will have the best farm stand ever," says Dad. Nora is missing 73 tomatoes. Matt is missing 55 peppers. Where did the vegetables go?

Farm Stand

Nora's tomatoes
  84 picked
 -11 left
  73 missing

Matt's peppers
  67 picked
 -12 left
  55 missing

9

Matt looks down the road. *Honk! Honk!*
A van is coming to the farm stand.

The van stops. Penny Porto jumps out. "Hello! What is wrong?" asks Penny.

Dad tells Penny that 73 tomatoes and 55 peppers are missing. Penny laughs and laughs. Penny opens the back of her van. The van is full of pizzas. Tomatoes and peppers cover the pizzas.

"What is funny?" asks Matt.

Penny says, "I was driving. I saw peppers and tomatoes fall off your truck. I honked. You did not stop. So I took the vegetables home. I made pizzas. I put the tomatoes and peppers on the pizzas."

"Can I sell my pizzas at your farm stand?" asks Penny.

"I do not know about that idea," says Dad.

Penny says, "I will share the money with you. I did use your vegetables."

"That idea is the best idea ever!" says Matt.

Nora says, "Please, Dad. The farm stand can be different this year."

Best Farm Stand

Pizza & Vegetables

15

People like the farm stand because it is different. Everyone comes to buy vegetables. People buy pizza with vegetables, too.

"The farm stand is the best ever!" says Dad.